Can Hens Give Milk?

Written By
JOAN BETTY STUCHNER

illustrated By
JOE WEISSMANN

ORCA BOOK PUBLISHERS

Library and Archives Canada Cataloguing in Publication

Stuchner, Joan Betty
Can hens give milk? / Joan Betty Stuchner ; illustrated by Joe Weissmann.

Issued also in electronic format.
ISBN 978-1-55469-319-1

I. Weissmann, Joe, 1947- II. Title.
PS8587.T825C35 2011   jc813'.54   C2010-907907-8

First published in the United States, 2011
Library of Congress Control Number: 2010941925

Summary: On a small farm in Chelm, a man and his daughter set out to find a way to get milk from their hens, and the results are not only funny, but also wacky.

Earlier versions of this story first appeared in *Spider Magazine* (May 2003), published by Carus Publishing Company, and also in a Scott Foresman Read Aloud Anthology for Grade 2 in the United States.

Orca Book Publishers is dedicated to preserving the environment and has printed this book on paper certified by the Forest Stewardship Council.

Orca Book Publishers gratefully acknowledges the support for its publishing programs provided by the following agencies: the Government of Canada through the Canada Book Fund and the Canada Council for the Arts, and the Province of British Columbia through the BC Arts Council and the Book Publishing Tax Credit.

Cover and interior artwork created using acrylic paints.

Cover artwork by Joe Weissmann
Design by Teresa Bubela

ORCA BOOK PUBLISHERS
PO Box 5626, Stn. B
Victoria, BC Canada
V8R 6S4

ORCA BOOK PUBLISHERS
PO Box 468
Custer, WA USA
98240-0468

www.orcabook.com
Printed and bound in Canada.

14 13 12 11 • 4 3 2 1

For the Children of
Temple Sholom
—J.B.S.

For my wife and children
—J.W.

A Note About Pronunciation

The "ch" in Chelm is pronounced like the
"ch" in the Scottish *loch* or the German *Bach*
(as if you're clearing your throat).

S hlomo and Rivka lived on a tiny farm in the town of Chelm. They had five children, twelve scrawny hens, one rooster and not much money.

One day Rivka said, "We have plenty of eggs from our hens, but if we owned a cow, we would also have milk and cheese."

Shlomo thought about what his wife had said.

That night he lay in bed and thought about it until he fell asleep.
Shlomo was a dreamer, and, sure enough, he had a dream. In his dream,
a cow was eating fresh green grass in their small field. Then he noticed
Rivka milking the cow.

Shlomo woke with a start and shouted, "That's it!"

His shouting woke Rivka. It also woke their six-year-old daughter, Tova.

Tova rushed into her parents' room. "What's wrong, Papa?"

"Let me ask you a question," said Shlomo. "Why does a cow give milk?"

"Everyone knows that, Papa. A cow gives milk because she eats grass."

Shlomo and Rivka beamed at their youngest daughter.

"What a wise child you are," said Shlomo. "So if we feed grass to our hens, they will still lay eggs, but they will also give us milk."

"Shlomo," said Rivka, "you are a genius."

"I am indeed," said Shlomo, and he blushed.

Tova yawned and went back to bed. Shlomo and
Rivka closed their eyes. They dreamed of fresh milk
and cheese. And as they slept, their mouths watered.

The next morning, Shlomo and Rivka tried to feed grass to their hens, but the hens refused. They ate only grain, as usual. Shlomo and Rivka were puzzled.

"A cow finds grass irresistible," said Rivka, "yet our foolish hens turn up their beaks in disgust. Why is that?"

Their four oldest children merely shrugged. But Tova said, "I know how to solve the problem, Papa. Roll the grass into pellets that look like grain. Then the hens will eat them."

Rivka clapped her hands. "Who would dare to say our little Tova does not have a wise head on her shoulders? She is a true daughter of Chelm."

Shlomo and Rivka rolled the grass into pellets. The children
scattered the pellets around the yard. Everyone watched and waited.
But still the hens only ate the grain.

"Tovaleh, you are smart," said Shlomo. "It's the hens who are stupid.
You must think of something else."

And she did.

Tova instructed her brothers and sisters to grab the hens.

The hens were not overjoyed. But as each hen opened its beak
to protest, Tova popped a pellet inside.

The hens clucked angrily, and the pellets gave them hiccups. "*Bock, bock, bock—hic. Bock, bock, bock—hic, hic*," they squawked as they ran back to the henhouse.

Shlomo was optimistic. "In the morning we will surely find our hens
have given us both eggs and milk."

Tova had one more thing to do before she went to bed. When everything
was quiet in the coop, she placed bowls beneath the sleeping hens.

All night long, Shlomo and his family
dreamed of milk and cheese.

The next morning, everyone rushed to the henhouse.

Shlomo and Tova lifted the hens.

They checked the bowls.

The bowls were empty!

Not only was there no milk, but none of the angry hiccupping hens had laid a single egg.

Shlomo scratched his head. "Such stubborn, foolish hens," he said. "What are we to do? Now we don't even have eggs for breakfast."

"Papa," said Tova, "I know someone who can help us. I'll be right back."

Tova soon returned with the wise Rabbi of Chelm.
Shlomo and Rivka led him to the henhouse.

The rabbi examined the hens one by one. He opened their beaks and looked down their throats.

He lifted them up and examined their feet. He scratched his head. He pulled on his beard.

"This is a puzzle," he said. "I'm not sure I can help you."

Tova had been watching the rabbi. And as she watched, she had an idea.

"Excuse me, Rabbi," said Tova. "Did you check underneath the hens?"

The rabbi looked down at little Tova and frowned. Then he put on his reading spectacles. He picked up a hen, turned it over and examined it more closely.

The rabbi's brows rose in amazement. He turned to Shlomo.
"Tova is a true daughter of Chelm."

"What do you mean?" said Rivka.

The rabbi showed Shlomo the hen's belly. "Look."

"What?" asked Shlomo. "There's nothing there."

"Exactly," said the rabbi. He pointed. "These hens have no udders.
They are just regular hens. They are not milk hens."

"No udders!" cried Shlomo. "Not milk hens!"

"I knew it was too good to be true," said Rivka.

The rabbi saw how disappointed they were. "I'll tell you what," he said. "I have two goats and one lonely rooster at home, but no hens. I will exchange one of my goats for six of your hens. Goats also give good milk. You shall have milk, and I shall have eggs."